Wee Donkey's Treasure Hunt

An Adventure around Ireland

Erika McGann

Gerry Daly

THE O'BRIEN PRESS

DUBLIN

For Beatrix - **EMcG**

*For Jutta - * **GD**

ERIKA McGANN is the author of numerous children's books,
including the picture book, *The Night Time Cat and the Plump,
Grey Mouse* (illustrated by Lauren O'Neill);
GERRY DALY is an illustrator from Dublin. Erika and Gerry's
previous picture book, the best-selling *Where Are You, Puffling?*,
is also published by The O'Brien Press.

First published 2020 by The O'Brien Press Ltd,
12 Terenure Road East, Rathgar, Dublin 6, D06 HD27, Ireland
Tel: +353 1 4923333; Fax: +353 1 4922777
E-mail: books@obrien.ie
Website: www.obrien.ie
The O'Brien Press is a member of Publishing Ireland.

Published in

DUBLIN
UNESCO
City of Literature

ISBN: 978-1-78849-180-8

8 7 6 5 4 3 2 1
23 22 21 20

Printed and bound in Poland by Białostockie Zakłady Graficzne S.A.
The paper in this book is produced using pulp from managed forests.

A wee donkey sat in the shade of a tree.
'If you had one wish, Grandad, what would it be?'
'I'd fix this old back and these wobbly knees,
and go see the sights that are out there to see.'

The wee donkey thought, 'I can't turn back the years,
but I can get Grandad some great souvenirs.'
She slipped through the gate with a small wooden cart,
in search of some gifts that would warm Grandad's heart.

First stop was a river, all busy and buzzing,
with people and sailors and boats by the dozen.
'These ships are so tall and their sails are so wide.
I'll just take this one and nobody will mind.'

The next spot was pretty, with lakes high and low,
wildlife to look at and places to go.

'Hmm,' said the donkey, 'I could take this flower,
but Grandad would love this gigantic round tower.'

In a beautiful garden, all misty and green,
sat a massive stone fort that was fit for a queen.
'The sign says this castle is crawling with witches,
but I think I'll take all these thousands of kisses.'

'How,' cried the donkey, 'did this come to be?

These stepping-stone sticks leading down to the sea!

Well, all of that rock would be heavy as lead.

I'll just take this one little giant instead.'

'Hey, look,' cried the donkey, 'there's books all around!'
But on seeing her cart, the librarian frowned.
'These books are all precious, they're not just for fun.'
'All right,' shrugged the donkey, 'I'll just take the one.'

JEANIE JOHNSTON

The Book of Kells

15

The wee donkey put on some fins and a tank,
and down to the depths of the ocean she sank.

'There's so many fish here, and all different kinds.

I'll just take the biggestest one I can find.'

The next place was ancient and brimming with magic.
'But Grandad won't see it, it's terribly tragic!'

Sunset Meeting 8 PM ish

Hill of Tara

The last souvenir that the wee donkey picked,
was a fairy who cried out, 'Oi help! I've been nicked!'

The donkey walked off with her cart full of loot,
and totally missed the gardaí in pursuit.
'Grandad!' she cried, with the guards close behind.
'I've brought you the best souvenirs I could find!'

'Now look here,' the guards said, 'you can't have this stuff. They're national treasures. Stop stealing. Enough!'

The wee donkey instantly thought of a plan.
'No problem,' she said, 'but can we use your van?'

They drove in the van 'cross the country, non-stop,
Grandad out the window, wee donkey on top.

They gave back the book,

and the tower of stone.

26

They gave back the kisses
(no witches were home).

They gave back the fairy, who yelled, 'About time!'

The biggestest fish flicked some seaweedy slime.

They put back the giant on stepping-stone sticks.

'Til finally, all that was left was the ship.

The wee donkey frowned then. 'I feel a bit sad,
that we've no souvenirs of the day that we've had.'

Her grandad just hugged her. 'My dear, that's not true.
I still have the best souvenir – I've got you.'